MW00904137

HAPPY EASTER
Bunny Express Mail

love

PLEASE DELIVER TO:

Hoppy The Easter

321 COTTONTAIL LANE
BUNNYVILLE, USA 10102

Dear Hoppy,

My name is _____. This year
I have been

- ☐ good
- ☐ helpful
- ☐ kind
- ☐ nice

Here is a drawing I made just for you.

Looking forward to your visit on Easter Sunday!

_____

Cut page from book. Trim envelope and fold on lines or cut out mailing address and tape to your own envelope. Insert letter and tape close. ✂

Hoppy The Easter Bunny

321 COTTONTAIL LANE
BUNNYVILLE, USA 10102

HAPPY EASTER
Bunny Express Mail

love

SPECIAL DELIVERY

_____

_____

_____

Hi There,

It's that time of year,

I am so excited to be hopping to your home on Easter Sunday
All year long the bunnies and
I have been coloring eggs and making Easter
baskets for each of our special friends.
This years basket is the best one yet.

A little bunny friend told me how good you have been.
I have a special basket that I'm filling just for you
with all kinds of yummy treats.
I can't wait to see how much you have grown this past year.
I remember when you were just a little baby snuggle bunny.

well I have to go for now looking forward
to a carrot or two when I reach your home.

I'm going to need all the
extra energy I can get to keep me
HOP. Hop. Hopping along
to all your friends and family.

Love ya,
Hoppy
The Easter Bunny

CERTIFICATE OF EGG-STRA GOOD BEHAVIOR

CONGRATULATIONS!

THIS IS TO CERTIFY THAT YOU HAVE BEEN

EGG-STRA GOOD THIS YEAR AND ARE

WORTHY OF MY SPECIAL GOLDEN EGG AWARD!

WELL DONE !!

Hoppy

Made in United States
Orlando, FL
10 April 2022

16683351R00018